FOSTER

by the same author

ANTARCTICA
WALK THE BLUE FIELDS

FOSTER

Claire Keegan

faber and faber

First published in 2010
by Faber and Faber Limited
Bloomsbury House
74–77 Great Russell Street
London WC1B 3DA

Typeset by Faber and Faber Limited
Printed and bound by CPI Group (UK) Ltd, Croydon, CR0 4YY

A CIP record for this book
is available from the British Library

ISBN 978–0–571–25565–8

For Ita Marcus
and in memory of David Marcus

I

Early on a Sunday, after first Mass in Clonegal, my father, instead of taking me home, drives deep into Wexford towards the coast where my mother's people came from. It is a hot day, bright, with patches of shade and greenish, sudden light along the road. We pass through the village of Shillelagh where my father lost our red Shorthorn in a game of forty-five, and on past the mart in Carnew where the man who won the heifer sold her shortly afterwards. My father throws his hat on the passenger seat, winds down the window, and smokes. I shake the plaits out of my hair and lie flat on the back seat, looking up through the rear window. In places there's a bare, blue sky. In places the blue sky is chalked over with clouds, but mostly it is a heady mixture of sky and trees scratched over by ESB wires across which, every now and then, small, brownish flocks of vanishing birds race.

I wonder what it will be like, this place belonging to the Kinsellas. I see a tall woman standing over me, making me drink milk still hot from the cow. I see another, less likely version of her in an apron, pouring pancake batter onto a frying pan, asking would I like another, the way my mother sometimes does when she is in good humour. The man will be her size. He will take me to town on the tractor and buy me red lemonade and crisps. Or he'll make me clean out sheds and pick stones and pull ragweed and docks out of the fields. I see him pulling what I hope will be a fifty-pence piece from his pocket but it turns out to be a handkerchief. I wonder if they live in an old farmhouse or a new bungalow, whether they will have an outhouse or an indoor bathroom with a toilet and running water. I picture myself lying in a dark bedroom with other girls, saying things we won't repeat when morning comes.

An age, it seems, passes before the car slows and turns into a tarred, narrow lane, then a thrill as the wheels slam over the metal bars of a cattle grid. On either side, thick hedges are trimmed square. At the end of the lane there's a long, white house with trees whose limbs are trailing the ground.

'Da,' I say. 'The trees.'

'What about 'em?'

'They're sick,' I say.

'They're weeping willows,' he says, and clears his throat.

In the yard, tall, shiny panes reflect our coming. I see myself looking out from the back seat wild as a tinker's child with my hair all loose but my father, at the wheel, looks just like my father. A big, loose hound whose coat is littered with the shadows of the trees lets out a few rough, half-hearted barks, then sits on the step and looks back at the doorway where the man

5

has come out to stand. He has a square body like the men my sisters sometimes draw, but his eyebrows are white, to match his hair. He looks nothing like my mother's people, who are all tall with long arms, and I wonder if we have not come to the wrong house.

'Dan,' he says, and tightens himself. 'What way are you?'

'John,' Da says.

They stand, looking out over the yard for a moment and then they are talking rain: how little rain there is, how the fields need rain, how the priest in Kilmuckridge prayed for rain that very morning, how a summer like it was never before known. There is a pause during which my father spits and then the conversation turns to the price of cattle, the EEC, butter mountains, the cost of lime and sheep-dip. It is something I am used to, this way men have of not talking: they like to kick a divot out of the grass with a boot heel, to slap the roof of a car before it takes off, to spit, to sit with their legs wide apart, as though they do not care.

When the woman comes out, she pays no heed to the men. She is even taller than my mother with the same black hair but hers is cut tight like a helmet. She's wearing a printed blouse and brown, flared trousers. The car door is opened and I am taken out, and kissed. My face, being kissed, turns hot against hers.

'The last time I saw you, you were in the pram,' she says, and stands back, expecting an answer.

'The pram's broken.'

'What happened at all?'

'My brother used it for a wheelbarrow and the wheel fell off.'

She laughs and licks her thumb and wipes something off my face. I can feel her thumb, softer than my mother's, wiping whatever it is away. When she looks at my clothes, I see my thin, cotton dress, my dusty sandals through her eyes. There's a moment when neither one of us knows what to say. A queer, ripe breeze is crossing the yard.

7

'Come on in, a Leanbh.'

She leads me into the house. There's a moment of darkness in the hallway; when I hesitate, she hesitates with me. We walk through into the heat of the kitchen where I am told to sit down, to make myself at home. Under the smell of baking there's some disinfectant, some bleach. She lifts a rhubarb tart out of the oven and puts it on the bench to cool: syrup on the point of bubbling over, thin leaves of pastry baked into the crust. A cool draught from the door blows in but here it is hot and still and clean. Tall ox-eyed daisies are still as the tall glass of water they are standing in. There is no sign, anywhere, of a child.

'So how is your mammy keeping?'

'She won a tenner on the prize bonds.'

'She did not.'

'She did,' I say. 'We all had jelly and ice cream and she bought a new tube and a mending kit for the bicycle.'

'Well, wasn't that a treat.'

'It was,' I say, and feel, again, the steel teeth of the comb against my scalp earlier that morning, the strength of my mother's hands as she wove the plaits tight, her belly at my back, hard with the next baby. I think of the clean pants she packed in the suitcase, the letter, and what she may have written. Words had passed between them:

'How long should they keep her?'

'Can't they keep her as long as they like?'

'Is that what I'll say?'

'Say what you like. Isn't it what you always do.'

Now, the woman fills an enamel jug with milk.

'Your mother must be busy.'

'She's waiting for them to come and cut the hay.'

'Have ye not the hay cut?' she says. 'Aren't ye late?'

When the men come in from the yard, it grows momentarily dark, then brightens once again when they sit down.

9

'Well, Missus,' says Da, pulling out a chair.

'Dan,' she says, in a different voice.

'There's a scorcher of a day.'

''Tis hot, surely.' She turns her back to watch the kettle, waiting.

'Wouldn't the fields be glad of a sup of rain,' he says.

'Won't we have the rain for long enough.' She looks at the wall as though a picture is hanging there but there is no picture on that wall, just a big mahogany clock with two hands and a big copper pendulum, swinging.

'Wasn't it a great year for the hay all the same. Never saw the like of it,' says Da. 'The loft is full to capacity. I nearly split my head on the rafters pitching it in.'

I wonder why my father lies about the hay. He is given to lying about things that would be nice, if they were true. Somewhere, further off, someone has started up a chainsaw and it drones on like a big, stinging wasp for a while in the distance. I wish I was out there, working. I am unused to sitting still and do not know what to do with my hands. Part of me wants my father to leave me here while another part of me wants him to take me back, to what I know. I am in a spot where I can neither be what I always am nor turn into what I could be.

The kettle lets off steam and rumbles up to boiling point, its steel lid clapping. The presence of a black-and-white cat moves on the window ledge. On the floor, across the hard, clean tiles, the woman's shadow stretches, almost reaching my chair. Kinsella gets up and takes a stack of plates from the cupboard, opens a drawer and takes out knives and forks, teaspoons. He takes the lid off a jar of beetroot and puts it on a saucer with a little serving fork, leaves out sandwich spread and salad cream. My father watches closely as he does this. Already there's a bowl of tomatoes and onions, chopped fine, a fresh loaf, a block of red cheddar.

'And what way is Mary?' the woman says.

'Mary? She's coming near her time.' Da sits back, satisfied.

'I suppose the last babby is getting hardy?'

'Aye,' Da says. 'It's the feeding them that's the trouble. There's no appetite like a child's and, believe you me, this one is no different.'

'Ah, don't we all eat in spurts, the same as we grow,' says the woman, as though this is something he should know.

'She'll ate but you can work her.'

Kinsella looks up. 'There'll be no need for any of that,' he says. 'The child will have no more to do than help Edna around the house.'

'We'll keep the child gladly,' the woman echoes. 'She's welcome here.'

'She'll ate ye out of house and home,' Da says, 'but I don't suppose there'll be a word about it this time twelve months.'

When we sit in at the table, Da reaches for the beetroot. He doesn't use the serving fork but pitches it onto the plate with his own. It stains the pink ham, bleeds. Tea is poured. There's a patchy silence as we eat, as our knives and forks break up what's on our plates. Then, after some time, the tart is cut. Cream falls over the hot pastry, into pools.

Now that my father has delivered me and eaten his fill, he is anxious to light his fag and get away. Always, it's the same: he never stays in any place long after he's eaten, not like my mother who would talk until it grew dark and light again. This, at least, is what my father says even though I have never known it to happen. With my mother it is all work: us, the butter-making, the dinners, the washing up and getting up and getting ready for Mass and school, weaning calves, and hiring men to plough and harrow the fields, stretching the money and setting the alarm. But this is a different type of house. Here there is room, and time to think. There may even be money to spare.

'I'd better hit the road,' Da says.

'What hurry is on you?' Kinsella says.

'The daylight is burning, and I've yet the spuds to spray.'

'There's no fear of blight these evenings,' the woman says, but she rises anyway, picks up the sharp knife and goes out the back door. I want to go with her, to shake the clay off whatever she cuts and carry it back into the house. A type of silence climbs and grows tall between the men while she is out.

'Give this to Mary,' she says, coming in. 'I'm snowed under with rhubarb, whatever kind of year it is.'

My father takes it from her but it is as awkward as the baby in his arms. A stalk falls to the floor and then another. He waits for her to pick it up, to hand it to him. She waits for him to do it. Neither one of them will budge. In the end, it's Kinsella who stoops to lift it.

'There now,' he says.

Out in the yard, my father throws the rhubarb onto the back seat, gets in behind the wheel and starts the engine.

'Good luck to ye,' he says. 'I hope this girl will give no trouble.' He turns to me then. 'Try not to fall into the fire, you.'

I watch him reverse, turn into the lane, and drive away. I hear the wheels slam over the cattle grid, then the changing of gears and the noise of the motor going back the road we came. Why did he leave without so much as a good-bye, without ever mentioning that he would come back for me? The strange, ripe breeze that's crossing the yard feels cooler now, and big white clouds have marched in across the barn.

'What's ailing you, Child?' the woman says.

I look at my feet, dirty in my sandals.

Kinsella stands in close. 'Whatever it is, tell us. We won't mind.'

'Lord God Almighty, didn't he go and forget all about your bits and bobs!' the woman says. 'No wonder you're in a state. Well, hasn't he a head like a sieve, the same man.'

'What matter,' Kinsella says. 'We'll have you togged out in no time.'

'There won't be a word about it this time twelve months,' the woman says.

They laugh hard for a moment then stop. When I follow the woman back inside, I want her to say something, to put my mind at ease. Instead, she clears the table, picks up the sharp knife and stands in the light under the window, washing the blade under the running tap. She stares at me as she wipes it clean, and puts it away.

'Now, Girleen,' she says. 'I think it's past time you had a bath.'

2

Beyond the kitchen, carpeted steps lead to an open room. There's a big double bed with a candlewick spread, and lamps at either side. This, I know, is where they sleep, and I'm glad, for some reason, that they sleep together. The woman takes me through to a bathroom, plugs a drain and turns the taps on full. The bath fills and the white room changes so that a type of blindness comes over us; we can see everything and yet we can't see.

'Hands up,' she says, and takes my dress off.

She tests the water and I step in, trusting her, but the water is too hot.

'Get in,' she says.

'It's too hot.'

'You'll get used to it.'

I put one foot through the steam and feel, again, the same rough scald. I keep my foot in the water, and then, when I think I can't stand it any longer, my thinking changes, and I can. This water is deeper than any I have ever bathed in. Our mother bathes us in what little she can, and makes us share. After a while, I lie back and through the steam watch the woman as she scrubs my feet. The dirt under my nails she prises out with tweezers. She squeezes shampoo from a plastic bottle, lathers my hair and rinses the lather off. Then she makes me stand and soaps me all over with a cloth. Her hands are like my mother's hands but there is something else in them too, something I have never felt before and have no name for. I feel at such a loss for words but this is a new place, and new words are needed.

'Now your clothes,' she says.

'I don't have any clothes.'

'Of course you don't.' She pauses. 'Would some of our old things do you for now?'

'I don't mind.'

'Good girl.'

She takes me to another bedroom past theirs, at the other side of the stairs, and looks through a chest of drawers.

'Maybe these will fit you.'

She is holding a pair of old-fashioned trousers and a new plaid shirt. The sleeves and legs are too long but she rolls them up, and tightens the waist with a canvas belt, to fit me.

'There now,' she says.

'Mammy says I have to change my pants every day.'

'And what else does your mammy say?'

'She says you can keep me for as long as you like.'

She laughs at this and brushes the knots out of my hair, and turns quiet. The windows in this room are open and through these I see a stretch of lawn, a vegetable garden, edible things growing in rows, red spiky dahlias, a crow with something in his beak which he slowly breaks in two and eats, one half and then the other.

'Come down to the well with me,' she says.

'Now?'

'Does now not suit you?'

Something about the way she says this makes me wonder if it's something we are not supposed to do.

'Is this a secret?'

'What?'

'I mean, am I not supposed to tell?'

She turns me round, to face her. I have not really looked into her eyes, until now. Her eyes are dark blue pebbled with other blues. In this light she has a moustache.

'There are no secrets in this house, do you hear?'

I don't want to answer back but feel she wants an answer.

'Do you hear me?'

'Yeah.'

'It's not "yeah". It's "yes". What is it?'

'It's yes.'

'Yes, what?'

'Yes, there are no secrets in this house.'

'Where there's a secret,' she says, 'there's shame, and shame is something we can do without.'

'Okay.' I take big breaths so I won't cry.

She puts her arm around me. 'You're just too young to understand.'

As soon as she says this, I realise she is just like everyone else, and wish I was back at home so that all the things I do not understand could be the same as they always are.

Downstairs, she fetches the zinc bucket from the scullery and takes me down the fields. At first I feel uneasy in the strange clothes but walking along I forget. Kinsella's fields are broad and level, divided in strips with electric fences she says I must not touch, unless I want a shock. When the wind blows, sections of the longer grass bend over, turning silver. On one strip of land, tall Friesian cows stand all around us, grazing. Some of them look up as we pass but not one of them moves away. They have huge bags of milk and long teats. I can hear them pulling the grass up from the roots. The breeze, crossing the rim of the bucket, whispers as we walk along. Neither one of us talks, the way people sometimes don't when they are happy. As soon as I have this thought I realise its opposite is also true. We climb over a stile and follow a dry path worn through the grass. The path snakes through a long field over which white butterflies skim and dart, and we wind up at a small iron gate where stone steps run down to a well. The woman leaves the bucket on the grass and comes down with me.

'Look,' she says, 'what water is here. Who'd ever think there wasn't so much as a shower since the first of the month?'

I go down steps until I reach the water. I breathe and hear the sound my breath makes over the still mouth of the well so I breathe harder for a while to feel these sounds I make, coming back. The woman stands behind, not seeming to mind each breath coming back, as though they are hers.

'Taste it,' she says.

'What?'

'Use the dipper.' She points.

Hanging over us is a big ladle, a shadow cupped in the dusty steel. I reach up and take it from the nail. She holds the belt of my trousers so I won't fall in.

'It's deep,' she says. 'Be careful.'

The sun, at a slant now, throws a rippled version of how we look back at us. For a moment, I am afraid. I wait until I see myself not as I was when I arrived, looking like a tinker's child, but as I am now, clean, in different clothes, with the woman behind me. I dip the ladle and bring it to my lips. This water is cool and clean as anything I have ever tasted: it tastes of my father leaving, of him never having been there, of having nothing after he was gone. I dip it again and lift it level with the sunlight. I drink six measures of water and wish, for now, that this place without shame or secrets could be my home. Then the woman pulls me back to where I am safe on the grass, and goes down alone. I hear the bucket floating on its side for a moment before it sinks and swallows, making a grateful sound, a glug, before it's torn away and lifted.

Walking back along the path and through the fields, holding her hand, I feel I have her balanced. Without me, I am certain she would tip over. I wonder how she manages when I am not here, and conclude that she must ordinarily fetch two buckets. I try to remember another time when I felt like this and am sad because I can't remember a time and happy, too, because I cannot.

That night, I expect her to make me kneel down but instead she tucks me in and tells me I can say a few little prayers in my bed, if praying is what I ordinarily do. The light of the day is still shining bright and strong. She is just about to hang a blanket over the curtain rail, to block it out, when she pauses.

'Would you rather I left it?'

'Yeah,' I say. 'Yes.'

'Are you afraid of the dark?'

I want to say I am afraid but am too afraid to say so.

'Never mind,' she says. 'It doesn't matter. You can use the toilet past our room but there's a chamber pot there too, if you'd prefer.'

'I'll be alright,' I say.

'Is your mammy alright?'

'What do you mean?'

'Your mammy. Is she alright?'

'She used to get sick in the mornings but now she doesn't.'

'Why isn't the hay in?'

'She hasn't enough to pay the man. She only just paid him for last year.'

'God help her.' She smoothes the sheet across me, pleats it. 'Do you think she would be offended if I sent her a few bob?'

'Offended?'

'Do you think she'd mind?'

I think about this for a while, think about being my mother. 'She wouldn't but Da would.'

'Ah yes,' she says. 'Your father.'

She leans over me then and kisses me, a plain kiss, and says good-night. I sit up when she is gone and look around the room. Trains of every colour race across the wallpaper. There are no tracks for these trains but here and there a small boy stands off in the distance, waving. He looks happy but some part of me feels sorry for every version of him. I roll onto my side and, though I know she wants neither, wonder if my mother will have a girl or a boy this time. I think of my sisters who will not yet be in bed. They will have thrown their clay buns against the gable wall of the outhouse, and when the rain comes, the clay will soften and turn to mud. Everything changes into something else, turns into some version of what it was before.

I stay awake for as long as I can, then make myself get up and use the chamber pot, but only a dribble comes out. I go back to bed, more than half afraid, and fall asleep. At some point later in the night – it feels much later – the woman comes in. I grow still and breathe as though I have not wakened. I feel the mattress sinking, the weight of her on the bed.

'God help you, Child,' she says. 'If you were mine, I'd never leave you in a house with strangers.'

3

I wake in this new place to the old feeling of being hot and cold, all at once. Mrs Kinsella does not notice until later in the day, when she is stripping the bed.

'Lord God Almighty,' she says.

'What?'

'Would you look?' she says.

'What?'

I want to tell her, right now, to admit to it and be sent home so it will be over.

'These old mattresses,' she says, 'they weep. They're always weeping. What was I thinking of, putting you on this?'

We drag it down the stairs, out into the sunlit yard. The hound comes up and sniffs it, ready to cock his leg.

'Get off, you!' she shouts in an iron voice.

'What's all this?' Kinsella has come in from the fields.

'It's the mattress,' she says. 'The bloody thing is weeping. Didn't I say it was damp in that room?'

'In fairness,' he says, 'you did. But you shouldn't have dragged that down the stairs on your own.'

'I wasn't on my own,' she says. 'I had help.'

We scrub it with detergent and hot water and leave it there in the sun to dry.

'That's terrible,' she says. 'A terrible start, altogether. After all that, I think we need a rasher.'

She heats up the pan and fries rashers and tomatoes cut in halves with the cut side down. She likes to cut things up, to scrub and have things tidy, and to call things what they are. 'Rashers,' she says, putting the rashers on the spitting pan. 'Run out there and pull a few scallions, good girl.'

I run out to the vegetable garden, pull scallions and run back in, fast as I can, as though the house is on fire and it's water I've been sent for. I'm wondering if there's enough but the woman laughs.

'Well, we'll not run short, anyhow.'

She puts me in charge of the toast, lighting the grill for me, showing how the bread must be turned when one side is brown, as though this is something I haven't ever done but I don't really mind; she wants me to get things right, to teach me.

'Are we ready?'

'Yeah,' I say. 'Yes.'

'Good girl. Go out there and give himself a shout.'

I go out and call the call my mother taught me, up the fields. 'Coo hooooooooooo!'

Kinsella comes in a few minutes later, laughing. 'Now there's a shout and a half,' he says. 'I doubt there's a child in Wexford with a finer set of lungs.' He washes his hands and dries them, sits in at the table and butters his bread. The butter is soft, slipping off the knife, spreading easily.

'They said on the early news that another striker is dead.'

'Not another?'

'Aye. He passed during the night, poor man. Isn't it a terrible state of affairs?'

'God rest him,' the woman says. 'It's no way to die.'

'Wouldn't it make you grateful, though?' he says. 'A man starved himself to death and here I am on a fine day wud two women feeding me.'

'Haven't you earned it?' the woman says.

'I don't know have I,' he says. 'But it's happening anyway.'

All through the day, I help the woman around the house. She shows me the big, white machine that plugs in, a freezer where what she calls 'perishables' can be stored for months without rotting. We make ice cubes, go over every inch of the floors with a hoovering machine, dig new potatoes, make coleslaw and two loaves, and then she takes the clothes in off the line while they are still damp and sets up a board and starts ironing. She is like the man, doing it all without rushing but neither one of them ever really stops. Kinsella comes in and makes tea for all of us and drinks it standing up with a handful of Kimberley biscuits, then goes back out again.

Later, he comes in looking for me.

'Is the wee girl there?' he calls.

I run out to the door.

'Can you run?'

'What?'

'Are you fast on your feet?' he says.

'Sometimes,' I say.

'Well, run down there to the end of the lane as far as the box and run back.'

'The box?' I say.

'The post box. You'll see it there. Be as fast as you can.'

I take off, racing, to the end of the lane and find the box and get the letters and race back. Kinsella is looking at his watch.

'Not bad,' he says, 'for your first time.'

He takes the letters from me. There's four in all, nothing in my mother's hand.

'Do you think there's money in any of these?'

'I don't know.'

'Ah, you'd know if there was, surely. The women can smell money. Do you think there's news?'

'I wouldn't know,' I say.

'Do you think there's a wedding invitation?'

I want to laugh.

'It wouldn't be yours anyhow,' he says. 'You're too young to be getting married. Do you think you'll get married?'

'I don't know,' I say. 'Mammy says I shouldn't take a present of a man.'

Kinsella laughs. 'She could be right there. Still and all, there's no two men the same. And it'd be a swift man that would catch you, Long

Legs. We'll try you again tomorrow and see if we can't improve your time.'

'I've to go faster?'

'Oh aye,' he says. 'By the time you're ready for home you'll be like a reindeer. There'll not be a man in the parish will catch you without a long-handled net and a racing bike.'

That night, after supper, when Kinsella is reading his newspaper in the parlour, the woman sits down at the cooker and tells me she is working on her complexion.

'It's a secret,' she says. 'Not many people know about this.'

She takes a packet of Weetabix out of the cupboard and eats one of them not with milk in a bowl but dry, out of her hand. 'Look at me,' she says. 'I haven't so much as a pimple.'

And sure enough, she doesn't. Her skin is clear.

'But you said there were no secrets here.'

'Ah, this is different, more like a secret recipe.'

She hands me one, then another and watches as I eat them. They taste a bit like the dry bark of a tree must taste but I don't really care, as some part of me is pleased to please her. I eat five in all during the nine o'clock news while they show the mother of the dead striker, a riot, then the Taoiseach and then foreign people out in Africa, starving to death, and then the weather forecast, which says the days are to be fine for another week or so. The woman sits me on her lap through it all and idly strokes my bare feet.

'You have nice long toes,' she says. 'Nice feet.'

Later, she makes me lie down on the bed before I go to sleep and cleans the wax out of my ears with a hair clip.

'You could have planted a geranium in what was there,' she says. 'Does your mammy not clean out your ears?'

'She hasn't always time,' I say, guarded.

'I suppose the poor woman doesn't,' she says. 'What with all of ye.'

She takes the hairbrush then and I can hear her counting under her breath to a hundred and then she stops and plaits it loosely. I fall asleep fast that night and when I wake, the old feeling is not there.

Later that morning, when Mrs Kinsella is making the bed, she looks at me, pleased.

'Your complexion is better already, see?' she says. 'All you need is minding.'

4

And so the days pass. I keep waiting for something to happen, for the ease I feel to end – to wake in a wet bed, to make some blunder, some big gaffe, to break something – but each day follows on much like the one before. We wake early with the sun coming in and have eggs of one kind or another with porridge and toast for breakfast. Kinsella puts on his cap and goes back out to the yard. Myself and the woman make a list out loud of jobs that need to be done, and just do them: we pull rhubarb, make tarts, paint the skirting boards, take all the bedclothes out of the hot press and hoover out the spider webs and put all the clean clothes back in again, make scones, scrub the bathtub, sweep the staircase, polish the furniture, boil onions for onion sauce and put it in containers in the freezer, pull the weeds out of the flower beds and then, when the sun goes down, water things. Then it's a matter of supper and the walk across the fields and to the well. Every evening the television is turned on for the nine o'clock news and then, after the forecast, I'm told it is time for bed.

Sometimes people come into the house at night. I can hear them playing cards and talking. They curse and accuse each other of reneging and dealing off the bottom, and coins are thrown into what sounds like a tin dish, and sometimes all the coins are emptied out into what sounds like a stash that's already there. Once somebody came in and played the spoons. Once there was something that sounded just like a donkey, and the woman came up to fetch me, saying I may as well come down, as nobody could get a wink of sleep with the Ass Casey in the house. I went down and ate macaroons and then two men came to the door selling lines for a raffle whose proceeds, they said, would go towards putting a new roof on the school.

'Of course,' Kinsella said.

'We didn't really think –'

'Come on in,' Kinsella said. 'Just 'cos I've none of my own doesn't mean I'd see the rain falling in on anyone else's.'

And so they came in and more tea was made and the woman emptied out the ashtray and dealt the cards and said she hoped the present generation of children in that school, if they were inclined towards cards, would learn the rules of forty-five properly because it was clear that this particular generation was having difficulties, that some people weren't at all clear on how to play, except for sometimes, when it suited them.

'Oh, there's shots!'

'You have to listen to thunder.'

'Aisy knowing whose purse is running low.'

'It's ahead, I am,' she said. 'And it's ahead I'll be when it's over.'

And this, for some reason, made the Ass Casey bray, which made me laugh and then they all started laughing until one of the men said, 'Is it a tittering match we have here or are we going to play cards?' which made the Ass Casey bray once more, and it started all over again.

5

One afternoon, while we are topping and tailing gooseberries for jam, when the job is more than half done and the sugar is already weighed and the pots warmed, Kinsella comes in from the yard and washes and dries his hands and looks at me in a way he has never done before.

'I think it's past time we got you togged out, Girl.'

I am wearing a pair of navy blue trousers and a blue shirt the woman took from the chest of drawers.

'What's wrong with her?' the woman says.

'Tomorrow's Sunday, and she needs something more than that for Mass,' he says. 'I'll not have her going as she went last week.'

'Sure isn't she clean and tidy?'

'You know what I'm talking about, Edna.' He sighs. 'Why don't you go up there and change and I'll run us all into Gorey.'

The woman keeps on picking the gooseberries from the colander, stretching her hand out, but a little more slowly each time, for the next one. At one point I think she will stop but she keeps on until she is finished and then she gets up and places the colander on the sink and lets out a sound I've never heard anyone make, and slowly goes upstairs.

Kinsella looks at me and smiles a hard kind of a smile then looks over to the window ledge where a sparrow has come down to perch and readjust her wings. The little bird seems uneasy – as though she can scent the cat, who sometimes sits there. Kinsella's eyes are not quite still in his head. It's as though there's a big piece of trouble stretching itself out in the back of his mind. He toes the leg of a chair and looks over at me.

'You should wash your hands and face before

42

you go to town,' he says. 'Didn't your father even bother to teach you that much?'

I freeze in the chair, waiting for something much worse to happen, but Kinsella does nothing more; he just stands there, locked in the wash of his own speech. As soon as he turns, I race for the stairs but when I reach the bathroom, the door won't open.

'It's alright,' the woman says, after a while, from inside and then, shortly afterwards, opens it. 'Sorry for keeping you.' She has been crying but she isn't ashamed. 'It'll be nice for you to have some clothes of your own,' she says then, wiping her eyes. 'And Gorey is a nice town. I don't know why I didn't think of taking you there before now.'

Town is a crowded place with a wide main street. Outside the shops, so many different things are hanging in the sun. There are plastic nets full of beach balls, blow-up toys. A see-through dolphin looks as though he is shivering in a cold breeze. There are plastic spades and matching buckets, moulds for sand castles, grown men digging ice cream out of tubs with little plastic spoons, potted plants that feel hairy to the touch, a man in a van selling dead fish.

Kinsella reaches into his pocket and hands me something. 'You'll get a Choc-ice out of that.'

I open my hand and stare at the pound note.

'Couldn't she buy half a dozen Choc-ices out of that,' the woman says.

'Ah, what is she for, only for spoiling?' Kinsella says.

'What do you say?' the woman says.

'Thanks,' I say. 'Thank you.'

'Well, stretch it out and spend it well,' Kinsella laughs.

The woman takes me to the draper's where she buys a packet of darning needles at a counter and four yards of oilcloth printed with yellow pears. Then we go upstairs where the clothing is kept. She picks out cotton dresses and some pants and trousers and a few tops and we go in behind a curtain so I can try them on.

'Isn't she tall?' says the assistant.

'We're all tall,' says the woman.

'She's the spit and image of her mammy. I can see it now,' the assistant says, and then says the lilac dress is the best fit and the most flattering, and the woman agrees. She buys me a printed blouse, too, with short sleeves much like the one she wore the day I came, dark blue trousers, and a pair of black leather shoes with a little strap and a buckle on the front, some panties and white ankle socks. The girl hands her the docket, and she takes out her purse and pays for it all.

'Well may you wear,' the assistant says. 'Isn't your mammy good to you?'

Out in the street, the sun feels strong again, blinding. Some part of me wishes it would go away, that it would cloud over so I could see properly. We meet people the woman knows.

Some of these people stare at me and ask who I am. One of them has a new baby in a push-chair. Mrs Kinsella bends down and coos and he slobbers a little and starts to cry.

'He's making strange,' the mother says. 'Pay no heed.'

We meet another woman with eyes like picks, who asks whose child I am, who I am belonging to? When she is told, she says, 'Ah, isn't she company for you all the same, God help you.'

Mrs Kinsella stiffens. 'You must excuse me,' she says, 'but this man of mine is waiting and you know what these men are like.'

'Like fecking bulls, they are,' the woman says. 'Haven't an ounce of patience.'

'God forgive me but if I ever run into that woman again it will be too soon,' says Mrs Kinsella, when we have turned the corner.

We go to the butchers for rashers and sausages and a horseshoe of black pudding, to the chemist where she asks for Aunt Acid, and then on down to a little shop she calls the gift gallery where they sell cards and notepaper and pretty pieces of jewellery from a case of revolving shelves.

'Isn't your mammy's birthday coming up shortly?'

'Yes,' I say, without being sure.

'We'll get a card for her, so.'

She tells me to choose, and I pick a card with a frightened-looking cat sitting in front of a bed of yellow dahlias.

'Not long now till they'll be back to school,' says the woman behind the counter. 'Isn't it a great relief to have them off your back?'

'This one is no trouble,' Mrs Kinsella says, and pays for the card along with some sheets of notepaper and a packet of envelopes. 'It's only missing her I'll be when she is gone.'

'Humph,' the woman says.

Before we go back to the car she lets me loose in a sweet shop. I take my time choosing, hand over the pound note and take back the change.

'Didn't you stretch it well,' she says, when I come out.

Kinsella is parked in the shade, with the windows open, reading the newspaper.

'Well?' he says. 'Did ye get sorted?'

'Aye,' she says.

'Grand,' he says.

I give him the Choc-ice and her the Flake and lie on the back seat eating the hard gums, careful not to choke as we cross over bumps in the road. I listen to the change rattling in my pocket, the wind rushing through the car and their talk, scraps of news being shared between them in the front.

When we turn into the yard, another car is parked outside the door. A woman is on the front step, pacing, with her arms crossed.

'Isn't that Harry Redmond's girl?'

'I don't like the look of this,' says Kinsella.

'Oh, John,' she says, rushing over. 'I'm sorry to trouble you but didn't our Michael pass away and there's not a soul at home. They're all out on the combines and won't be back till God knows what hour and I've no way of getting word to them. We're rightly stuck. Would you ever come down and give us a hand digging the grave?'

'I don't know that this'll be any place for you but I can't leave you here,' the woman says, later that same day. 'So get ready and we'll go, in the name of God.'

I go upstairs and change into the new dress, the ankle socks and shoes.

'Don't you look nice,' she says, when I come down. 'John's not always easy but he's hardly ever wrong.'

Walking down the road, there's a taste of something darker in the air, of something that might come and fall and change things. We pass houses whose doors and windows are wide open, long, flapping clotheslines, gravelled entrances to other lanes. At the bend, a bay pony is leaning up against a gate, but

when I reach out to stroke his nose, he whin-
nies and canters off. Outside a cottage, a black
dog with curls all down his back comes out
and barks at us, hotly, through the bars of a
gate. At the first crossroads, we meet a heifer
who panics and finally races past us, lost. All
through the walk, the wind blows hard and
soft and hard again through the tall, flower-
ing hedges, the high trees. In the fields, the
combines are out cutting the wheat, the barley
and oats, saving the corn, leaving behind long
rows of straw. We meet men on tractors, going
in different directions, pulling balers to the
fields, and trailers full of grain to the co-op.
Birds swoop down, brazen, eating the fallen
seed off the middle of the road. Further along,
we meet two barechested men, their eyes so
white in faces so tanned and dusty.

The woman stops to greet them and tells
them where we are going.

'God rest him. Didn't he go quick in the
end?' one man says.

'Aye,' says the other. 'But didn't he reach his three score and ten? What more can any of us hope for?'

We keep on walking, standing in tight to the hedges, the ditches, letting things pass.

'Have you been to a wake before?' the woman asks.

'I don't think so.'

'Well, I might as well tell you: there will be a dead man here in a coffin and lots of people and some of them might have a little too much taken.'

'What will they be taking?'

'Drink,' she says.

When we come to the house, several men are leaning against a low wall, smoking. There's a black ribbon on the door and hardly a light shining from the house but when we go in, the kitchen is bright, and packed with people who are talking. The woman who asked Kinsella to dig the grave is there, making sandwiches. There are big bottles of red and white lemonade, stout, and in the middle of all this, a big wooden box with an old dead man lying inside of it. His hands are joined as though he had died praying, a string of rosary beads around his fingers. Some of the men are sitting around the coffin, using the part that's closed as a counter on which to rest their glasses. One of these is Kinsella.

'There she is,' he says. 'Long Legs. Come over here.'

He pulls me onto his lap, and gives me a sip from his glass.

'Do you like the taste of that?'

'No.'

He laughs. 'Good girl. Don't ever get a taste for it. If you start, you might never stop and then you'd wind up like the rest of us.'

He pours red lemonade into a cup for me. I sit on his lap drinking it and eating the queen cakes out of the biscuit tin and looking at the dead man, hoping his eyes will open.

The people come and go, drifting in and out, shaking hands, drinking and eating and looking at the dead man, saying what a lovely corpse he is, and doesn't he look happy now that his end has come, and who was it that laid him out? They talk of the forecast and the moisture content of corn, of milk quotas and the next general election. I feel myself getting heavy on Kinsella's lap.

'Am I getting heavy?'

'Heavy?' he says. 'You're like a feather, Child. Stay where you are.'

I put my head against him but I'm bored and wish there were things to do, other children who would play.

'The girl's getting uneasy,' I hear the woman say.

'What's ailing her?' says another.

'Ah, it's no place for the child, really,' she says. 'It's just I didn't like not to come, and I wouldn't leave her behind.'

'Sure I'll take her home with me, Edna. I'm going now. Can't you call in and collect her on your way?'

'Oh,' she says. 'I don't know should I.'

'Mine'd be a bit of company for her. Can't they play away out the back? And that man there won't budge as long as he has her on his knee.'

Mrs Kinsella laughs. I've never heard her laugh like this.

'Sure maybe, if you don't mind, you would, Mildred,' she says. 'What harm is in it? And you know we'll not be long after you.'

'Not a bother,' the woman says.

When we are out on the road, and the good-byes are said, Mildred strides on into a pace I can just about keep, and as soon as she rounds the bend, the questions start. She is eaten alive with curiosity; hardly is one question answered before the next is fired: 'Which room did they put you into? Did Kinsella give you money? How much? Does she drink at night? Does he? Are they playing cards up there much? Who was there? What were they selling the lines for? Do ye say the rosary? Does she put butter

54

or margarine in her pastry? Where does the old dog sleep? Is the freezer packed solid? Does she skimp on things or is she allowed to spend? Are the child's clothes still hanging in the wardrobe?'

I answer them all easily, until the last.

'The child's clothes?'

'Aye,' she says. 'Sure if you're sleeping in his room you must surely know. Did you not look?'

'Well, she had clothes I wore for all the time I was here but we went to Gorey this morning and bought all new things.'

'This rig-out you're wearing now? God Almighty,' she says. 'Anybody would think you were going on for a hundred.'

'I like it,' I say. 'They told me it was flattering.'

'Flattering, is it? Well. Well,' she says. 'I suppose it is, after living in the dead's clothes all this time.'

'What?'

'The Kinsellas' young lad, you dope. Did you not know?'

I don't know what to say.

'That must have been some stone they rolled back to find you. Sure didn't he follow that auld hound of theirs into the slurry tank and drown? That's what they say happened anyhow,' she says.

I keep on walking and try not to think about what she has said even though I can think of little else. The time for the sun to go down is getting close but the day feels like it isn't ending. I look at the sky and see the sun, still high, and clouds, and, far away, a round moon coming out.

'They say John got the gun and took the hound down the field but he hadn't the heart to shoot him, the softhearted fool.'

We walk on between the bristling hedges in which small things seem to rustle and move. Chamomile grows along these ditches, wood sage and mint, plants whose names my mother somehow found the time to teach me. Further along, the same lost heifer is still lost, in a different part of the road.

'And you know, the pair of them turned white overnight.'

'What do you mean?'

'Their hair, what else?'

'But Mrs Kinsella's hair is black.'

'Black? Aye, black out of the dye-pot, you mean.' She laughs.

I wonder at her laughing like this. I wonder at the clothes and how I'd worn them and the boy in the wallpaper and how I never put it all together. Soon we come to the place where the black dog is barking through the bars of the gate.

'Shut up and get in, you,' she says to him.

It's a cottage she lives in with uneven slabs of concrete outside the front door, overgrown shrubs, and tall Red Hot Pokers growing out of the ground. Here I must watch my head, my step. When we go in, the place is cluttered and an older woman is smoking at the cooker. There's a baby in a high chair. He lets out a cry when he sees the woman and drops a handful of marrowfat peas over the edge.

'Look at you,' she says. 'The state of you.'

I'm not sure if it's the woman or the child she is talking to. She takes off her cardigan and sits down and starts talking about the wake: who was there, the type of sandwiches that were made, the queen cakes, the corpse who was lying up crooked in the coffin and hadn't even been shaved properly, how they had plastic rosary beads for him, the poor fucker.

I don't know whether to sit or stand, to listen or leave but just as I'm deciding what to do, the dog barks and the gate opens and Kinsella comes in, stooping under the door frame.

'Good evening all,' he says.

'Ah, John,' the woman says. 'You weren't long. We're only in the door. Aren't we only in the door, Child?'

'Yes.'

Kinsella hasn't taken his eyes off me. 'Thanks, Mildred. It was good of you, to take her home.'

'It was nothing,' the woman says. 'She's a quiet young one, this.'

'She says what she has to say, and no more. May there be many like her,' he says. 'Are you ready to come home, Petal?'

I get up and he talks on a little, to smooth things over, the way people do. I follow him out to the car where the woman is waiting.

'Were you alright in there?' she says.

I say I was.

'Did she ask you anything?'

'A few things, nothing much.'

'What did she ask you?'

'She asked me if you used butter or margarine in your pastry.'

'Did she ask you anything else?'

'She asked me was the freezer packed tight.'

'There you are,' says Kinsella.

'Did she tell you anything?' the woman asks.

I don't know what to say.

'What did she tell you?'

'She told me you had a little boy who followed the dog into the slurry tank and died, and that I wore his clothes to Mass last Sunday.'

When we get home, the hound gets up and comes out to the car to greet us. It's only now I realise I've not heard either one of them call him by his name. Kinsella sighs and goes off to milk. When he comes inside, he says he's not ready for bed and that there will be no visitors tonight anyhow, on account of the wake – not, he says, that he wants any. The woman goes upstairs and changes and comes back down in her nightdress. Kinsella has taken my shoes off and has put what I now know is the boy's jacket on me.

'What are you doing now?' she says.

'What does it look like? And she'll break her neck in these.'

He goes out, stumbling a little, then comes back in with a sheet of sandpaper and scuffs up the soles of my new shoes so I will not slip.

'Come on,' he says. 'We'll break them in.'

'Didn't she already break them in? Where are you taking her?'

'Only as far as the strand,' he says.

'You'll be careful with that girl, John Kinsella,' she says. 'And don't you go without the lamp.'

'What need is there for a lamp on a night like tonight?' he says but he takes it anyhow, as it's handed to him.

There's a big moon shining on the yard, chalking our way onto the lane and along the road. Kinsella takes my hand in his. As soon as he takes it, I realise my father has never once held my hand, and some part of me wants Kinsella to let me go so I won't have to feel this. It's a hard feeling but as we walk along I begin to settle and let the difference between my life at home and the one I have here be. He takes small steps so we can walk in time. I think about the woman in the cottage, of how she walked and spoke, and conclude that there are huge differences between people.

When we reach the crossroads we turn right, down a steep, sloping road. The wind is high and hoarse in the trees, tearing fretfully through the dry boughs, when their leaves rise and swing. It's sweet to feel the open road falling away under us, knowing we will, at its end, come to the sea. The road goes on and the sky, everything, seems to get brighter. Kinsella says a few meaningless things along the way then falls into the quiet way he has about him, and time passes without seeming to pass and then we are in a sandy, open space where people must park cars. It is full of tyre marks and potholes, a rubbish bin which seems not to have been emptied in a long time.

'We're almost there now, Petal.'

He leads me up a steep hill where, on either side, tall rushes bend and shake. My feet sink in the deep sand, and the climb takes my breath away. Then we are standing on the crest of a dark place where the land ends and there is a long strand and water which I know is deep and stretches all the way to England. Far out, in the darkness, two bright lights are blinking.

Kinsella lets me loose and I race down the far side of the dune to the place where the black sea hisses up into loud, frothy waves. I run towards them as they back away and run back, shrieking, when another crashes in. When Kinsella catches up, we take our shoes off. In places we walk along with the edge of the sea clawing at the sand under our bare feet. In places he leaves me to run. At one point we go in until the water is up to his knees and he holds me on his shoulders.

'Don't be afraid!' he says.

'What?'

'Don't be afraid!'

The strand is all washed clean, without so much as a footprint. Beyond a crooked line in the sand, close to the dunes, things have washed up: plastic bottles, sticks, the handle of a mop whose head is lost and, further on, a stable door, whose bolt is broken.

'Some man's horse is loose tonight,' Kinsella says. He walks on for a while then. It is quieter up here, away from the noise of the waves. 'You know the fishermen sometimes find horses out at sea. A man I know towed a colt in one time and the horse lay down for a long time before he got up. And he was perfect. Tiredness was all it was, after being out so long.

'Strange things happen,' he says. 'A strange thing happened to you tonight but Edna meant no harm. It's too good, she is. She wants to find the good in others, and sometimes her way of finding that is to trust them, hoping she'll not be disappointed but she sometimes is.'

He laughs then, a queer, sad laugh. I don't know what to say.

'You don't ever have to say anything,' he says. 'Always remember that as a thing you need never do. Many's the man lost much just because he missed a perfect opportunity to say nothing.'

Everything about the night feels strange: to walk to a sea that's always been there, to see it and feel it and fear it in the half dark, and to listen to this man saying things about horses out at sea, about his wife trusting others so she'll learn who not to trust, things I don't fully understand, things which may not even be intended for me.

We keep on walking until we come to a place where the cliffs and rocks come out to meet the water. Now that we can go no farther, we must turn back. Maybe the way back will somehow make sense of the coming. Here and there, flat white shells lie shining and washed up on the sand. I stoop to gather them. They feel smooth and clean and brittle in my hands. We turn back along the beach and walk on, seeming to walk a greater distance than the one we crossed in reaching the place where we could not pass, and then the moon disappears behind a darkish cloud and we cannot see where we are going. At this point, Kinsella lets out a sigh, stops, and lights the lamp.

'Ah, the women are nearly always right, all the same,' he says. 'Do you know what the women have a gift for?'

'What?'

'Eventualities. A good woman can look far down the line and smell what's coming before a man even gets a sniff of it.'

He shines the light along the strand to find our footprints, to follow them back, but the only prints he can find are mine.

'You must have carried me there,' he says.

I laugh at the thought of me carrying him, at the impossibility, then realise it was a joke, and that I got it.

When the moon comes out again, he turns the lamp off and by the moon's light we easily find and follow the path we took out of the dunes. When we reach the top, he won't let me put my shoes on but does it for me. Then he does his own and knots the laces. We stand then, to pause and look back out at the water.

'See, there's three lights now where there was only two before.'

I look out across the sea. There, the two lights are blinking as before, but with another, steady light, shining there also.

'Can you see it?' he says.

'I can,' I say. 'It's there.'

And that is when he puts his arms around me and gathers me into them as though I were his.

6

After a week of rain, on a Thursday, the letter comes. It is not so much a surprise as a shock. Already I have seen the signs: the shampoo for head lice in the chemist's shop, the fine-tooth combs. In the gift gallery there are copy books stacked high and different coloured biros, rulers, mechanical drawing sets. In the hardware, the lunchboxes and satchels and hurling sticks are left out front, where the women can see them.

We come home and take soup, dipping our bread, breaking it, slurping a little, now that we know each other. Afterwards, I follow Kinsella out to the hayshed where he makes me promise not to look while he is welding. I am following him around today, I realise, but I cannot help it.

It is past the time for the post to come but he does not suggest I fetch it until evening, until the cows are milked and the milking parlour is swept and scrubbed.

'I think it's time,' he says, washing his boots with the hose.

I get into position, using the front step as a starting block. Kinsella looks at the watch and slices the air with his hand. I take off, down the yard, the lane, make a tight corner, open the box, reach for the letters, and race back to the step, knowing my time was not as fast as yesterday's.

'Nineteen seconds faster than your first run,' Kinsella says. 'And a two-second improvement on yesterday, despite the heavy ground. It's like the wind, you are.'

He takes the letters and goes through them, but today, instead of making jokes about what's inside of each, he pauses.

'Is that from Mammy?'

'You know,' he says, 'I think it could be.'

'Do I have to go home?'

'Well, it's addressed to Edna so why don't we give it in to her and let her read it.'

We go into the parlour where she is sitting with her feet up, looking through a book of knitting patterns. There's a coal fire in the grate, and little plumes of black smoke sliding back down into the room.

'This chimney, we never got it cleaned, John. I'm sure there must be a crow's nest in it.'

Kinsella slides the letter onto her lap, over what she is reading. She sits up, opens the letter and reads it. It's one small sheet with writing on both sides. She puts it down then picks it up and reads it again.

'Well,' she says, 'you have a new brother. Nine pounds, two ounces.'

'Great,' I say.

'Don't be like that,' Kinsella says.

'What?' I say.

'And school starts on Monday,' she says. 'Your mother has asked us to leave you up at the weekend so she can get you togged out and all.'

'I have to go back then?'

'Aye,' she says. 'But sure didn't you know that?'

I nod and look at the page in her lap.

'You couldn't stay here forever with us two old forgeries.'

I stand there and stare at the fire, trying not to cry. It is a long time since I have done this and, in doing it, remember that it is the worst thing you can possibly do. I don't so much hear as feel Kinsella leaving the room.

'Don't upset yourself,' the woman says. 'Come over here.'

She shows me pages with knitted jumpers and asks me which pattern I like best, but all the patterns seem to blur together and I just point to one, a blue one, which looks like it might be easy.

'Well, you would pick the hardest one in the book,' she says. 'I'd better get started on that this week or you'll be too big for it by the time it's knitted.'

7

Now that I know I must go home, I almost want to go, to get it over with. I wake earlier than usual and look out at the wet fields, the dripping trees, the hills, which seem greener than they did when I came. I think back to this time and it seems so long ago, when I used to wet the bed and worry about breaking things. Kinsella hangs around all day doing things but not really finishing anything. He says he has no discs for his angle grinder, no welding rods, and he cannot find the vice grip. He says he got so many jobs done in the long stretch of fine weather that there's little left to do.

We are out looking at the calves, who are feeding. With warm water, Kinsella has made up their milk replacement which they suck from long, rubber teats until the teats run dry. It's an odd system, taking the calves off the cows and giving them milk replacement so Kinsella can milk their mothers and sell the milk, but they look content.

'Could ye leave me back this evening?'

'This evening?' Kinsella says.

I nod.

'Any evening suits me,' he says. 'I'll take you whenever you want, Petal.'

I look at the day. The day is like any other, with a flat grey sky hanging over the yard and the wet hound on watch outside the front door.

'Well, I had better milk early, so,' he says. 'Right,' and goes on down the yard past me as though I have already gone.

The woman gives me a brown leather bag. 'You can keep this old thing,' she says. 'I never have use for it.'

We fold my clothes and place them inside, along with the books we bought at Webb's in

73

Gorey: *Heidi*, *What Katy Did Next*, *The Snow Queen*. At first, I struggled with some of the bigger words but Kinsella kept his fingernail under each, patiently, until I guessed it and then I did this by myself until I no longer needed to guess, and read on. It was like learning to ride the bike; I felt myself taking off, the freedom of going places I couldn't have gone before, and it was easy.

Mrs Kinsella gives me a bar of yellow soap and my facecloth, the hairbrush. As we gather all these things together, I remember the days we spent, where we got them, what was some-times said, and how the sun, for most of the time, was shining.

Just then a car pulls into the yard. It's a neighbouring man I remember from the night of cards.

'Edna,' he says in a panic. 'Is John about?'

'He's out at the milking,' she says. 'He should be finishing up now.'

He runs down the yard, heavy in his Wellington boots, and a minute later, Kinsella sticks his head around the door.

'Joe Fortune needs a hand pulling a calf,' he says. 'Would you ever just finish the parlour off? I have the herd out.'

'I will, surely,' she says.

'I'll be back just as soon as I can.'

'Don't I know you will.'

She puts on her anorak and goes down the yard to the milking parlour. I sit restless and wonder should I go out to help but come to the conclusion that I'd only be in the way. So I sit in the armchair and look out to where a watery light is trembling across the scullery, shining off the zinc bucket. I could go down to the well for water so she would have the well water for her tea when she gets back home tonight. It could be the last thing I do.

I put on the boy's jacket and take up the bucket and walk down the fields. I know the way along the track and past the cows, the electric fences, could find the well with my eyes closed. When I cross the stile the path does not look like the same path we followed on that first evening here. The way is muddy now and slippery in places. I trudge along, towards the little iron gate and down the steps. The water is much higher these days. I was on the fifth step that first evening here, but now I stand on the first and see the edge of the water reaching up and just about sucking the edge of the step that's one down from me. I stand there breathing, making the sounds for a while to hear them coming back, one last time. Then I bend down with the bucket, letting it float then swallow and sink as the woman does but when I reach out with my other hand to lift it, another hand just like mine seems to come out of the water and pull me in.

8

It is not that evening or the following one but the evening after, on the Sunday, that I am taken home. After I came back from the well, soaked to the skin, the woman took one look at me and turned very still before she gathered me up and took me inside and made up my bed again. The following morning, I didn't feel hot, but she kept me upstairs, bringing me hot drinks with lemon and cloves and honey, aspirin.

"Tis nothing but a chill, she has,' I heard Kinsella say.

'When I think of what could have happened.'

'If you've said that once, you've said it a hundred times.'

'But –'

'Nothing happened, and the girl is grand. And that's the end of it.'

I lie there with the hot-water bottle, listening to the rain and reading my books, following what happens more closely and making up something different to happen at the end of each, each time. I doze and have strange dreams: of the lost heifer panicking on the night strand, of bony, brown cows having no milk in their teats, of my mother climbing up and getting stuck in an apple tree. Then I wake and take the broth and whatever else I'm given.

On Sunday, I am allowed to get up, and we pack everything again, as before. Towards evening, we have supper, and wash and change into our good clothes. The sun has come out, is lingering in long, cool slants, and the yard is dry in places. Sooner than I would like, we are ready and in the car, turning down the lane, going up through the street of Gorey and on back along the narrow roads through Carnew and Shillelagh.

'That's where Da lost the red heifer playing cards,' I say.

'Is that a fact?' Kinsella says.

'Wasn't that some wager?' says the woman.

'It was some loss for him,' says Kinsella.

We carry on through Parkbridge, over the hill where the old school stands, and on down towards our car-road. The gates in the lane are closed and Kinsella gets out to open them. He drives through, closes the gates behind him, and drives on very slowly to the house. I feel, now, that the woman is making up her mind as to whether or not she should say something but I don't really know what it is, and she gives me no clue. The car stops in front of the house, the dogs bark, and my sisters race out. I see my mother looking out through the window, with what is now the second youngest in her arms.

Inside, the house feels damp and cold. The lino is all tracked over with dirty footprints.

Mammy stands there with my little brother, and looks at me.

'You've grown,' she says.

'Yes,' I say.

'"Yes", is it?' she says, and raises her eyebrows.

She bids the Kinsellas good evening and tells them to sit down – if they can find a place to sit – and fills the kettle from the bucket under the kitchen table. We take playthings off the car seat under the window, and sit down. Mugs are taken off the dresser, a loaf of bread is sliced, butter and jam left out.

'Oh, I brought you jam,' the woman says. 'Don't let me forget to give it to you, Mary.'

'I made this out of the rhubarb you sent down,' Ma says. 'That's the last of it.'

'I should have brought more,' the woman says. 'I wasn't thinking.'

'Where's the new addition?' Kinsella asks.

'Oh, he's up in the room there. You'll hear him soon enough.'

'Is he sleeping through the night for you?'

'On and off,' Ma says. 'The same child could crow at any hour.'

My sisters look at me as though I'm an English cousin, coming over to touch my dress, the buckles on my shoes. They seem different, thinner, and have nothing to say. We sit in to the table and eat the bread and drink the tea. When a cry is heard from upstairs, Ma gives my brother to Mrs Kinsella, and goes up to fetch the baby. The baby is pink and crying, his fists tight. He looks bigger than the last, stronger.

'Isn't there a fine child, God bless him,' Kinsella says.

'Isn't he a dote,' Mrs Kinsella says, holding on to the other.

Ma pours more tea for them all with one hand and sits down and takes her breast out for the baby. Her doing this in front of Kinsella makes me blush. Seeing me blush, Ma gives me a long, deep look.

'No sign of himself?' Kinsella says.

'He went out there earlier, wherever he's gone,' Ma says.

A little bit of talk starts up then, rolls back and forth, bumping between them for a while. Soon after, a car is heard outside. Nothing more is said until my father appears, and throws his hat on the dresser.

'Evening all,' he says.

'Dan,' says Kinsella.

'Ah there's the prodigal child,' he says. 'You came back to us, did you?'

I say I did.

'Did she give trouble?'

'Trouble?' Kinsella says. 'Good as gold, she was, the same girl.'

'Is that so?' says Da, sitting down. 'Well, isn't that a relief.'

'You'll want to sit in,' Mrs Kinsella says, 'and get your supper.'

'I had a liquid supper,' Da says, 'down in Parkbridge.'

Ma turns the baby to the other breast, and

changes the subject. 'Have ye no news at all from down your way?'

'Not a stem,' says Kinsella. 'It's all quiet down with us.'

I sneeze then, and reach into my pocket for my handkerchief, and blow my nose.

'Have you caught cold?' Ma asks.

'No,' I say, hoarsely.

'You haven't?'

'Nothing happened.'

'What do you mean?'

'I didn't catch cold,' I say.

'I see,' she says, giving me another deep look.

'The child's been in the bed for the last couple of days,' says Kinsella. 'Didn't she catch herself a wee chill.'

'Aye,' says Da. 'You couldn't mind them. You know yourself.'

'Dan,' Ma says, in a steel voice.

Mrs Kinsella looks uneasy, like she was the day of the gooseberries.

'You know, I think it's nearly time that we

were making tracks,' Kinsella says. 'It's a long road home.'

'Ah, what's the big hurry?' Ma says.

'No hurry at all, Mary, just the usual. These cows don't give you any opportunity to have a lie-in.'

He gets up then and takes my little brother from his wife and gives him to my father. My father takes the child and looks across at the baby suckling. I sneeze and blow my nose again.

'That's a right dose you came home with,' Da says.

'It's nothing she hasn't caught before and won't catch again,' Ma says. 'Sure isn't it going around?'

'Are you ready for home?' Kinsella asks.

Mrs Kinsella stands then and they say their good-byes and go outside. I follow them out to the car with my mother who still has the baby in her arms. Kinsella lifts out the box of jam, the four-stone sack of potatoes.

'These are floury,' he says. 'Queens they are, Mary.'

We stand for a little while and then my mother thanks them, saying it was a lovely thing they did, to keep me.

'No bother at all,' says Kinsella.

'The girl was welcome and is welcome again, any time,' the woman says.

'She's a credit to you, Mary,' Kinsella says. 'You keep your head in the books,' he says to me. 'I want to see gold stars on them copy books next time I come up here.' He gives me a kiss then and the woman hugs me and then I watch them getting into the car and feel the doors closing and a start when the engine turns and the car begins to move away. Kinsella seems more eager to leave than he was in coming here.

'What happened at all?' Ma says, now that the car is gone.

'Nothing,' I say.

'Tell me.'

'Nothing happened.' This is my mother I am speaking to but I have learned enough, grown enough, to know that what happened is not something I need ever mention. It is my perfect opportunity to say nothing.

I hear the car braking on the gravel in the lane, the door opening, and then I am doing what I do best. It's nothing I have to think about. I take off from standing and race on down the lane. My heart does not so much feel that it is in my chest as in my hands, and that I am carrying it along swiftly, as though I have become the messenger for what is going on inside of me. Several things flash through my mind: the boy in the wallpaper, the gooseberries, that moment when the bucket pulled me under, the lost heifer, the mattress weeping, the third light. I think of my summer, of now, mostly of now.

As I am rounding the bend, reaching the point where I daren't look, I see him there, putting the clamp back down on the gate, closing it. His eyes are down, and he seems to be looking at his hands, at what he is doing. My feet batter on along the rough gravel, along the strip of tatty grass in the middle of our lane. There is only one thing I care about now, and my feet are carrying me there. As soon as he sees me he stops and grows still. I do not hesitate but keep on running towards him and by the time I reach him the gate is open and I am smack against him and lifted into his arms. For a long stretch, he holds me tight. I feel the thumping of my heart, my breaths coming out then my heart and my breaths settling differently. At a point, which feels much later, a sudden gust blows through the trees and shakes big, fat raindrops over us. My eyes are closed and I can feel him, the heat of him coming through his good clothes. When I finally open my eyes and look over his shoulder, it is my father I see, coming along strong and steady, his walking stick in his hand. I hold on as though I'll drown if I let go, and listen to the woman who seems, in her throat, to be taking it in turns, sobbing and crying, as though she is crying not for one now, but for two. I daren't keep my eyes open and yet I do, staring up the lane, past Kinsella's shoulder, seeing what he can't. If some part of me wants with all my heart to get down and tell the woman who has minded me so well that I will never, ever tell, something deeper keeps me there in Kinsella's arms, holding on.

'Daddy,' I keep calling him, keep warning him. 'Daddy.'

Acknowledgements

The author would like to thank Richard Ford for all his kindness; Declan Meade of *The Stinging Fly*, and Redmond Doran of Davy Byrne's pub who sponsored the award.

ff

Faber and Faber is one of the great independent publishing houses. We were established in 1929 by Geoffrey Faber with T. S. Eliot as one of our first editors. We are proud to publish award-winning fiction and non-fiction, as well as an unrivalled list of poets and playwrights. Among our list of writers we have five Booker Prize winners and twelve Nobel Laureates, and we continue to seek out the most exciting and innovative writers at work today.

Find out more about our authors and books
faber.co.uk

Read our blog for insight and opinion on books and the arts
thethoughtfox.co.uk

Follow news and conversation
twitter.com/faberbooks

Watch readings and interviews
youtube.com/faberandfaber

Connect with other readers
facebook.com/faberandfaber

Explore our archive
flickr.com/faberandfaber